This book belongs to

. . . .

Pocket Treasury

EGMONT

We bring stories to life

This edition published in 2012 by Dean,
an imprint of Egmont UK Limited
239 Kensington High Street, London W8 6SA

Thomas the Tank Engine & Friends™

CREATED BY BRITT ALLCROFT

HiT entertainment

ISBN 978 0 6035 6674 5
49671/1
Printed in Singapore

Pocket Treasury

DEAN

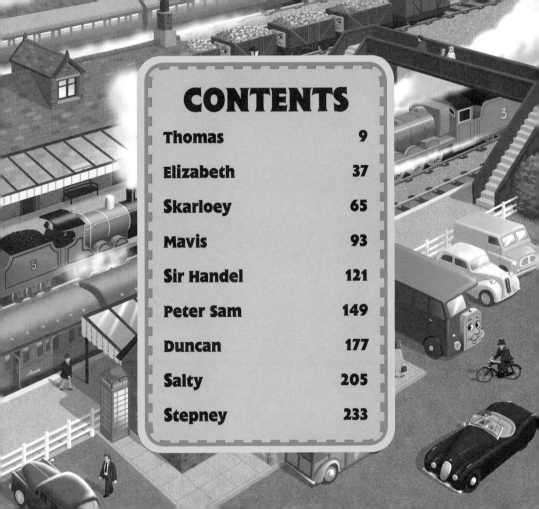

CONTENTS

THOMAS

Based on *The Railway Series* by the Rev. W. Awdry

Illustrations by

Robin Davies and Jerry Smith

TO THE TRAINS ➜

*T*his is a story about Thomas
the Tank Engine. Thomas worked
really hard, shunting coaches
for the big engines. But what
he wanted more than
anything was his very
own branch line . . .

Thomas the Tank Engine had six small wheels, a short stumpy funnel, a short stumpy boiler and a short stumpy dome. He was a fussy little engine, always pulling coaches about. He pulled them to the station ready for the big engines to take out on journeys; and when trains came in, he pulled the empty coaches away so that the big engines could have a rest.

But what Thomas really wanted was his very own branch line. That way he would be a Really Useful Engine.

Thomas was a cheeky little engine. He thought no engine worked as hard as he did, and he liked playing tricks on the others.

One day, Gordon had just returned from pulling the big Express. He was very tired, and had just gone to sleep when Thomas came up beside him:

"WAKE UP, LAZYBONES!" whistled Thomas. "Do some hard work for a change!" And he ran off, laughing.

Gordon got a terrible shock. He decided he had to pay Thomas back.

The next morning, Thomas wouldn't wake up. His Driver and Fireman couldn't make him start. It was nearly time for Gordon's Express to leave. Gordon was waiting, but Thomas hadn't got his coaches ready.

At last Thomas started. "Oh dear! Oh dear!" he yawned.

"Poop! Poop! Poop! Hurry up, you!" said Gordon crossly.

"Peep! Peep! Peep! Hurry up yourself!" replied Thomas, cheekily.

Thomas usually pushed behind Gordon's train to help him start. But he was always uncoupled first, so that when the train was running nicely Thomas could stop and go back.

That morning, Gordon saw the perfect chance to pay Thomas back for giving him a fright. He started so quickly that the Guards forgot to uncouple Thomas.

Gordon moved slowly out of the station, pulling the train and Thomas with him. Then he started to go faster and faster – much too fast for Thomas!

"Peep! Peep! Stop! Stop!" whistled Thomas.

"Hurry, hurry, hurry, hurry!" laughed Gordon in front.

"You can't get away. You can't get away," giggled the coaches.

Poor Thomas was going faster than he had ever gone before. "I shall never be the same again," he thought, sadly. "My wheels will be quite worn out."

At last they stopped at a station. Thomas was uncoupled and given a long, long drink.

"Well, little Thomas," chuckled Gordon. "Now you know what hard work, means, don't you?"

Poor Thomas was too breathless to answer.

The next day, Thomas was working in the Yard. On a siding by themselves were some strange-looking trucks.

"That's the breakdown train," said his Driver. "When there's an accident, the workmen use it to help clear and mend the line."

Just then, James came whistling through the Yard crying, "Help! Help!" His brake blocks were on fire and his trucks were pushing him faster and faster.

James disappeared into the distance.

Soon after, a bell rang in the signal box and a man came running.

"James is off the line! We need the breakdown train – quickly!" he shouted.

Thomas was coupled on to the breakdown train, and off he went as fast as he could.

"Bother those trucks and their tricks!" he said. "I hope James isn't hurt."

They found James and the trucks at a bend in the line. James was in a field, with a cow staring at him. The brake van and the last few trucks were still on the rails, but the front ones were piled in a heap behind James.

James' Driver and Fireman were checking to see if he was hurt. "Don't worry, James," his Driver said. "It wasn't your fault – it was those Troublesome Trucks."

Thomas pushed the breakdown train alongside James, then he pulled the trucks that were still on the line out of the way.

"Oh . . . dear! Oh . . . dear!" they groaned.

"Serves you right. Serves you right,"
puffed Thomas, crossly.

As soon as the other trucks were back on the line, Thomas pulled them away, too. He was hard at work all afternoon.

Using two cranes, the men put James carefully back on the rails. He tried to move, but he couldn't, so Thomas pulled him back to the shed.

The Fat Controller was waiting for them there.

"Well, Thomas," he said kindly, "I've heard all about it and I think you're a Really Useful Engine. I'm so pleased with you, that I'm going to give you your own branch line."

"Oh, thank you, Sir!" said Thomas, happily.

Now Thomas is as content as can be.
He has a branch line all to himself, and he puffs
proudly backwards and forwards from morning
till night, with his coaches Annie and Clarabel.

Edward and Henry stop quite often at the
junction to talk to him.

Gordon is always in a hurry and does not stop,
but he never forgets to say, "Poop! Poop! Poop!"
to Thomas; and Thomas always whistles,
"Peep! Peep! Peep!" in return.

ELIZABETH

Based on *The Railway Series* by the Rev. W. Awdry

Illustrations by

Robin Davies and Jerry Smith

TO THE TRAINS →

This is a story about Elizabeth the Vintage Sentinel Lorry. Sadly, she was left to rust in a shed for a long time. Find out what happened when Thomas' Driver found her there . . .

Thomas was taking heavy goods trucks to a cargo ship at Brendam Docks. The ship was leaving at sundown, so Thomas had to work hard to get the trucks there in time.

Suddenly, one of his coupling rods broke.

His Driver saw a shed by the track.
"I'll see if there are some tools in there," he said.

"Be careful! That shed looks a bit spooky," said Thomas.

Then a voice came from inside the shed: "Be quiet out there, I'm trying to sleep!" Thomas' Driver went into the shed. After a few moments, he came out again.

"Well? Is it a ghost?" asked Thomas.

"No!" laughed his Driver, "It's not a ghost. It's a very helpful surprise."

Thomas' Driver and Fireman took coal into the shed. Thomas wondered what they were doing.

"She should be able to get us to the fitter's yard," Thomas heard his Driver say.

"If her boiler holds," replied his Fireman. "She badly needs repair work."

Thomas heard lots of clanking noises coming from the shed. What could be inside?

At last, out of the shed drove a rather dirty, old steam lorry.

"Thomas, this is Elizabeth," said his Driver.

"So you're the little puffer that has broken down," said Elizabeth to Thomas.

Thomas didn't like that at all. "You're a rude, old steam lorry!" he replied, sharply.

"Actually, I'm a Vintage Sentinel Lorry," replied Elizabeth. "And you should be thankful that I'm here to help you!"

Elizabeth and Thomas' Driver went to the fitter's yard. Elizabeth's engine made loud grinding noises. As she drove up a steep hill, her engine got louder and louder.

"You're not built for hills," said Thomas' Driver. "Will you make it?"

"I'll be fine," replied Elizabeth. "I'm just catching my breath."

Before long, Elizabeth reached the fitter's yard. Thomas' Driver fetched a new coupling rod and they drove back to Thomas.

Elizabeth felt very proud. She realised she had been in the shed for so long that she had forgotten how much fun it was to help others.

Thomas was impressed with how quickly Elizabeth had fetched the coupling rod. He was about to thank her, when she said, "Next time, make sure you're not so careless!"

Now Thomas thought Elizabeth was the rudest lorry he had ever met! He waited in silence while his Driver fitted the new coupling rod, then he set off to the Docks.

Elizabeth decided to follow Thomas to the Docks. "That little puffer has already broken one coupling rod, so he may well need my help again!" she thought.

Elizabeth's engine rattled and groaned as she slowly followed behind Thomas. Soon Thomas was out of sight, but Elizabeth didn't mind. She remembered which roads she had to take to get to the Docks.

Thomas arrived at the Docks just in time. As the goods were unloaded from his trucks, The Fat Controller came over. He looked very cross indeed.

"Where have you been?" he asked. "You nearly missed the boat!"

Thomas told him about his broken coupling rod. He was about to tell him about Elizabeth, when she drove up!

"Oh! It's you!" said Elizabeth to The Fat Controller. "Have you learnt how to drive properly yet?"

Thomas thought The Fat Controller would be very angry, but to his surprise The Fat Controller said, "Elizabeth! The first lorry I ever drove. How marvellous to see you again! Where have you been?"

Thomas couldn't believe it – Elizabeth and The Fat Controller were friends!

Elizabeth told The Fat Controller that she had been left in the shed a long time ago and everyone had forgotten about her. She had thought she would never drive again.

The Fat Controller was really pleased that Elizabeth had been found. He asked Jem Cole, the mechanic, to restore her to her original beauty. Elizabeth smiled happily and thanked The Fat Controller. She could hardly wait to be in full working order again.

A few weeks later, Elizabeth drove past The Fat Controller's station. Her paintwork shone and her engine sounded perfect.

"Hello," she said. "Don't you think my new paintwork looks marvellous?"

"You're the grandest lorry in the whole railroad!" replied The Fat Controller.

Thomas had to agree. And Elizabeth was so happy now she was useful again, that she wasn't rude at all!

SKARLOEY

Based on *The Railway Series* by the Rev. W. Awdry

Illustrations by

Robin Davies and Phil Jacobs

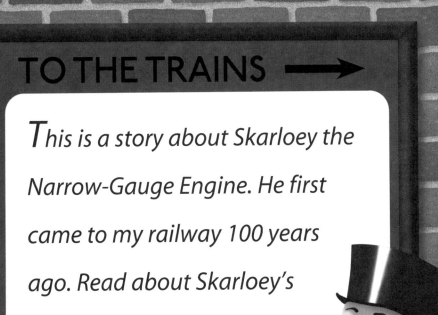

TO THE TRAINS ➡

This is a story about Skarloey the Narrow-Gauge Engine. He first came to my railway 100 years ago. Read about Skarloey's troubles when he was brand new – and couldn't stop bouncing up and down!

Skarloey worked on the Little Railway, on the Island of Sodor.

He was 100 years old, but he was still a Useful Engine. All the other engines liked Skarloey and he would tell them stories about when he was young.

Everyone's favourite story was about the time Skarloey first came to the Little Railway.

Skarloey was built at the same time as another engine called Rheneas. They were both red, with four wheels each.

"We look wonderful," said Skarloey, proudly.

"We will pull coaches and everyone will want to ride in them!" replied Rheneas.

Skarloey and Rheneas were both going to work on the mountain line of the Little Railway. But Skarloey was finished first, so he had to go to the Little Railway alone, leaving Rheneas behind. The two engines felt sad when they said goodbye to each other.

Skarloey was sent away on a ship.

At the port they used the ship's cranes to lift Skarloey on to the shore. The ship's cranes were called 'derricks', and they nearly turned Skarloey upside down.

"How dare they treat me like this!" said Skarloey, crossly.

He was left hanging from the derricks for a long time. At last an engine arrived to take him to the mountain line.

"About time!" huffed Skarloey.

It was dark when Skarloey arrived at the mountain line. He felt lonely and miserable. "I wish Rheneas was here," he said, sadly.

Next morning there were trucks everywhere. They rattled and roared past Skarloey.

"There's no engine pulling them!" said Skarloey in surprise.

"The trucks come down the mountain by gravity," explained the Manager. "But the empty ones need taking up again. That's why you've come."

"What?" said Skarloey, crossly. "I don't want to pull trucks! Can't I pull coaches, Sir?"

"Certainly not," said the Manager. "We have to finish building this line, and for that, we need trucks. The Inspector is coming to look at the line soon."

Skarloey was furious. When the workmen tried to start him, his fire wouldn't burn. He made no steam – he just blew smoke at them. They tried again the next day, and the next, and the next. But Skarloey wouldn't do a thing!

Finally, the Manager lost his temper. "We're not going to look at your sulky face all day, Skarloey," he said. "We'll leave you alone until you're a better engine."

They covered Skarloey with a big sheet of tarpaulin and went away. Skarloey felt even more lonely and unhappy. Nobody talked to him.

At last the Manager came back. "I hope that you will be a better engine from now on," he said.

"Yes Sir, I will Sir!" said Skarloey, earnestly.

From then on, Skarloey worked very hard, and although he sometimes got too excited and would bounce up and down, the Manager was very pleased with his efforts.

By the time Rheneas arrived at last, the line was ready. Skarloey was delighted to see his old friend!

Rheneas soon settled in. One day, while he was shunting trucks, Skarloey hurried up to him. "I'm going to pull the Inspector's train, today!" said Skarloey.

"Be careful not to bounce," said Rheneas. "The Inspector won't like that."

But Skarloey was so excited, he just couldn't stop bouncing!

Skarloey had to take the Inspector up to the top of the mountain, and then back down again.

The upward journey went well and Skarloey felt very happy.

When it was time to go down, Skarloey was really excited. As they went faster and faster, he began to bounce! The coaches were scared. "He's playing tricks!" they said. "Bump him! Bump him!"

Just then, Skarloey gave an extra big bounce, and the Inspector lost his footing. He flew into a bush on the side of the line!

The Driver stopped the train. The Inspector was not hurt, but he was very cross!

"From now on, you will stay in the shed!" he said to Skarloey. "You are a bad engine!"

When the Inspector told the Manager what had happened, the Manager felt sorry for Skarloey. He knew that he had been trying very hard to be good.

"What Skarloey needs is an extra pair of wheels," he said. "Then he won't bounce any more." So Skarloey was sent off to the Works.

When Skarloey came back, Rheneas hardly recognised him. He had six wheels and a brand new cab, and he looked very smart.

"Now let's see what you can do," said the Manager. Sure enough, Skarloey found it much easier to travel along smoothly, without bouncing.

From then on, Skarloey pulled coaches and trucks up and down the track easily and he didn't bounce his passengers once! And 100 years later, he is still as good as new!

MAVIS

Based on *The Railway Series* by the Rev. W. Awdry

Illustrations by

Robin Davies and Creative Design

TO THE TRAINS ➡

This is a story about Mavis the Diesel Engine. Mavis worked at the Quarry, shunting trucks. She was bored with her job, until one day she was given the chance to make it more exciting . . .

Mavis was a diesel engine who worked at the Quarry. She shunted trucks for other engines to collect.

Mavis was a young engine, and she liked to get her own way. She thought she knew better than everyone else.

Every day, Mavis would put Toby's trucks in a different place, so he had to search for them.

"Trucks should be where I can find them," said Toby, crossly.

"Nonsense!" said Mavis.

"I can't waste time arguing!" said Toby. "If you know so much, then take the trucks yourself!"

Mavis was very pleased. Taking trucks on Toby's branch line made her feel important.

So the next day, Mavis set off along the branch line with Toby's trucks. But the trucks didn't like bossy Mavis.

"It's frosty today. Let's play a trick on her!" they whispered.

Mavis travelled happily along Toby's line. Ahead of her was a level crossing, so she stopped carefully. "I'm so good at this. I don't need silly old Toby!" she laughed.

But she didn't know what the trucks were planning.

When it was time to move again, the trucks whispered to each other, "Hold back! Hold back!"

Mavis tried to set off, but her wheels just spun. She couldn't get a grip on the frosty ground. The Troublesome Trucks giggled and giggled.

The drivers of the cars and lorries waiting at the level crossing were getting very angry. But there was nothing Mavis could do!

Then Mavis saw Toby approaching in the distance. He had come to help.

"Having trouble, Mavis?" he smiled.

Mavis felt cross and silly. She had boasted to Toby that she knew best, and now she was stuck and Toby had to rescue her!

Toby was coupled to Mavis. He puffed and slipped, and at last he got Mavis and the trucks moving. Mavis hardly helped at all. She didn't even say 'thank you'.

When Mavis got back to the Quarry,
The Fat Controller was very cross with her.

"You are a naughty engine," he said.
"You will stay here in future!"

Mavis felt angry. She thought the Quarry was
boring. She wished she could go on Toby's
branch line again.

Soon spring arrived on Sodor. It was a very busy time at the Quarry. Every day, Mavis got the trucks ready for Toby. But she was never allowed to take them along Toby's branch line.

Then one day, Mavis had an idea. She said to the Troublesome Trucks: "When we get to the beginning of Toby's line, please will you bump me? Then I'll be on his line whether he likes it or not!"

"Yes! Yes! Yes!" giggled the trucks.

"I'll show that fusspot Toby," said Mavis to herself.

But when the time came, Mavis was busy elsewhere, so Toby shunted the trucks himself.

"Never mind," the trucks whispered to each other. "Let's bump Toby instead!"

So they gave Toby a big bump! He rushed on to his branch line much too fast. His Driver and Fireman were knocked over. Toby was out of control!

Toby couldn't stop! He rushed over the level crossing. Luckily there weren't any cars there.

Up ahead there was an old bridge. The river had flooded and part of the bridge had been washed away.

If Toby didn't stop before he reached it, he might fall in the river!

As Toby approached the bridge, the rails stretched across the gap, just like a tightrope!

His Driver braked hard but Toby slid along the track. His brakes squealed. He used every bit of his strength and stopped . . . just in time!

Mavis felt terrible. It was all her fault! So she rushed to the rescue. First she pulled the trucks back up the track. Then she helped pull Toby carefully away from the bridge.

"I'm sorry, Toby!" she said. "It's all my fault!"

"Never mind, Mavis," said Toby, kindly. "Thank you for rescuing me!"

After that day, Mavis and Toby became good friends. Mavis still bossed the trucks around at the Quarry, but she always listened to Toby's advice.

And sometimes, for a special treat, Toby would let Mavis take the trucks carefully along his branch line!

SIR HANDEL

Based on *The Railway Series* by the Rev. W. Awdry

Illustrations by

Robin Davies and Creative Design

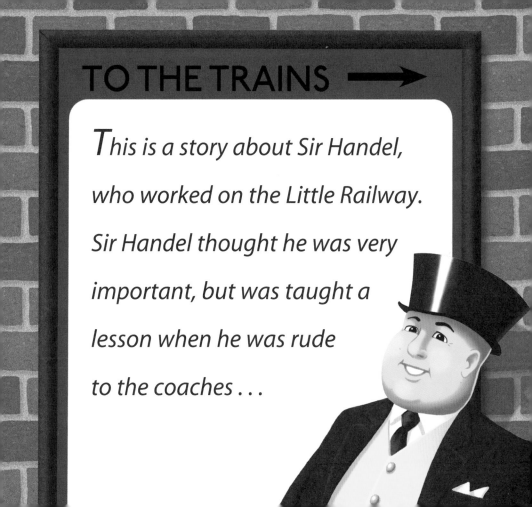

TO THE TRAINS ➡

This is a story about Sir Handel, who worked on the Little Railway. Sir Handel thought he was very important, but was taught a lesson when he was rude to the coaches . . .

Skarloey and Rheneas worked on the Little Railway. But they were growing old and tired, so The Thin Controller (who ran the Little Railway) brought two more engines to help them.

The new engines looked very smart! One was called Peter Sam and the other was called Sir Handel.

"What a small shed!" grumbled Sir Handel, when he saw his new home. "This won't do at all."

"I think it's nice," said Peter Sam.

"Humph!" replied Sir Handel. "And what's that pile of rubbish over there?"

"Shhh," replied Peter Sam. "That's Skarloey, the famous old engine!"

The next morning, the Fireman came to get Sir Handel ready for his first day's work.

"I'm tired," yawned Sir Handel. "Can Peter Sam go instead? He likes hard work – I don't know why."

"No," said the Fireman. "It's The Thin Controller's orders. You're first!"

Sir Handel's Driver arrived, and they set off to fetch the coaches.

But when Sir Handel saw them, he screeched to a standstill.

"They're not coaches!" he said. "They're so old and dirty, they look like cattle trucks!"

The five coaches – Agnes, Ruth, Lucy, Jemima and Beatrice – were very offended! "Ooooooh!" they screamed. "What a horrid engine!"

Sir Handel was coupled to the coaches, and set off towards the station. He rolled on to the platform just as Gordon arrived.

"Hello!" said Sir Handel. "Who are you?"

"I'm Gordon," said Gordon. "Who are you?"

"I'm Sir Handel. I've heard of you, you're an Express engine, I believe. So am I, but I'm used to proper coaches – not these cattle trucks. Anyway, sorry, can't stop – must keep time, you know!"

And Sir Handel puffed off!

"Come along! Come along!" puffed Sir Handel to the coaches, as he pulled them along.

The coaches were very angry because Sir Handel had called them names.

"Cattle trucks! Cattle trucks!" they grumbled. "We'll pay him back! We'll pay him back!"

Soon they came to a station. Beyond it, the line curved, then began to climb. The day was misty and the rails were slippery.

Suddenly, Agnes had an idea.

"Hold back!" she whispered to Ruth.

"Hold back!" whispered Ruth to Lucy.

"Hold back!" whispered Lucy to Jemima.

"Hold back!" whispered Jemima to Beatrice.

The coaches giggled as Sir Handel started and their couplings tightened.

"Come on! Come on!" puffed Sir Handel as his wheels slipped on the greasy rails. He started to climb the hill, but the coaches pulled him back and the train ground to a halt.

"I can't do it! I can't do it!" Sir Handel grumbled. "I'm used to sensible coaches, not these cattle trucks!"

The Guard came up. "I think the coaches are up to something," he told the Driver. So they decided to bring the train down again to a level piece of line, to give Sir Handel a good start.

The Guard and the Fireman sanded the rails and Sir Handel made a tremendous effort. The coaches tried hard to drag him back, but he puffed and pulled so hard that they were soon over the hill and away on their journey.

That night, The Thin Controller spoke to Sir Handel. "You are a Troublesome Engine," he said. "You are much too big for your wheels!"

"But those coaches were misbehaving," said Sir Handel. "They tried to stop me climbing the hill!"

"That is no surprise," said The Thin Controller, "considering how rude you were to them. You will pull trucks in the Quarry until you have learned to behave better!"

"TRUCKS?" cried Sir Handel.

Sir Handel had to shunt trucks in the Quarry for a whole week. The trucks were troublesome and would not do as they were told.

At the end of the week, Sir Handel was a much better behaved engine.

"Are you ready to pull coaches again?" asked The Thin Controller.

"Oh, yes please, Sir!" replied Sir Handel.

He set off to fetch his coaches and was determined to be much nicer to them.

When the coaches saw him, they muttered to each other, "Grumpy Sir Handel! Grumpy Sir Handel!" They were sure he was going to be rude again.

But Sir Handel was as polite as could be. He was coupled to the coaches and set gently off down the branch line.

And from that day on, Sir Handel tried very hard to behave. He knew he would rather pull coaches that looked like cattle trucks, than shunt real trucks in the Quarry!

PETER SAM

Based on *The Railway Series* by the Rev. W. Awdry

Illustrations by

Robin Davies and Jerry Smith

TO THE TRAINS ➡

This is a story about Peter Sam, a Narrow-Gauge Engine. He first worked at the Old Railway for The Thin Controller many years ago. Everyone made fun of his new funnel, but he soon had the last laugh . . .

It was winter on the Island of Sodor. Peter Sam was puffing slowly along the track.

He was worried about his funnel. It had not felt right since he had had an accident with some trucks, and now it felt like the wind was trying to blow it off.

"My funnel feels all wobbly," he said to his Driver. "I wish my new one would hurry up and arrive. The Thin Controller said it will be something special!"

"You and your special funnel," laughed Rusty, Sir Handel and Duncan. They all liked Peter Sam but his special funnel had become a bit of a joke.

The winter wind grew stronger and rain lashed down on the engines. The heavy rain turned the hillside streams into raging rivers which threatened to wash away the tracks.

Rusty worked hard carrying workmen up and down the line to clear the branches and leaves so the water could flow away from the tracks.

The next day, Rusty's Driver brought bad news. "There's been a washout near the tunnel," he said. "The track bed has been swept away. We need to repair it immediately!"

The repair work took much longer than expected. As the days went by, the weather became much colder and frosty. Finally, the repairs were finished so the tunnel could be used again.

The next morning, Peter Sam carefully went over the mended track and slowly rolled into the dark tunnel.

His Driver shouted, "There's something hanging from the roof!"

There was a loud clanging noise and Peter Sam suddenly felt rather strange. As he came out of the tunnel, his Driver saw that he had lost his funnel!

Peter Sam's Guard went back into the tunnel to find his funnel. He came out holding the funnel and a large icicle.

"This is what hit you!" he said. "We can't mend your funnel here, we'll have to finish the journey without it and get it repaired at the station."

Peter Sam set off again but, without his funnel, smoke billowed over the carriages and the passengers complained.

At the side of the track, his Driver noticed an old drainpipe. He wired it to Peter Sam to work as a funnel for the rest of the journey. Peter Sam was embarrassed.

"I hope none of the other engines see me looking like this," he said sadly.

But as Peter Sam approached the station, Rusty and Sir Handel saw his drainpipe funnel. They burst into laughter and sang a song:

"Peter Sam's said again and again,
His new funnel will put ours to shame.
But he went into a tunnel,
And lost his old funnel,
Now his famous special funnel's a drain!"

Luckily for Peter Sam, his new funnel had arrived that day. He couldn't wait to see it, but when his Driver opened the parcel he thought there had been a mistake.

"Oh, no! Has somebody squashed my new funnel?" asked Peter Sam.

The Thin Controller laughed. "Don't worry," he said. "It's a special funnel, called a Giesl. It is the most up-to-date funnel there is!"

"How does it work?" asked Peter Sam.

"When you puff, you draw air through your fire to make it burn brightly. Your old funnel made puffing hard work, but your new Giesl funnel has special pipes to help the air come easily. You'll now have more strength to do your work."

Peter Sam wasn't sure that he was going to like having the strange new funnel.

At first, the other engines thought Peter Sam's new funnel was a great joke.

"Did you sit on it?" asked Duncan and hooted with laughter.

"It's certainly *special!*" giggled Sir Handel.

Peter Sam had wished he had his old funnel back but he soon realized that The Thin Controller had been right. His new funnel did make work much easier. Now the other engines would have nothing to laugh about.

Peter Sam became very proud of his new funnel. It helped him glide along the tracks, easily pulling long lines of trucks behind him.

Sir Handel, Duncan and Rusty soon stopped laughing at his new funnel. They watched in amazement as he sped past them, pulling more trucks than he had ever been able to before. The other engines wished they also had a special funnel just like Peter Sam!

DUNCAN

Based on *The Railway Series* by the Rev. W. Awdry

Illustrations by

Robin Davies and Jerry Smith

TO THE TRAINS ⟶

This is a story about Duncan the Narrow-Gauge Engine. Duncan used to complain about his passengers. But this changed when Skarloey told a story about how Rheneas saved the Railway …

One morning, Skarloey was in the Yard, being polished by Nancy, the Guard's daughter.

Skarloey was thinking about his friend Rheneas, who had gone away to be mended.

"Rheneas comes home tomorrow," said Nancy.

"What? Tomorrow?" chirped Skarloey. "I must look my very best! Please polish me some more!"

"You're such an old fuss pot!" laughed Nancy.

Duncan was jealous. "Aren't you going to polish me, too?" he asked.

"Sorry, I have to get the ice lollies ready for the passengers," said Nancy.

"It's not fair," Duncan complained. "Peter Sam gets a new funnel, Skarloey gets special wheels, passengers get ice lollies, but I'm not even polished!"

Duncan enjoyed complaining and he soon began to sulk.

That afternoon, there was bad news from up the line.

"One of Skarloey's coaches has derailed," called Duncan's Driver. "We'll have to go there right away."

Duncan took the workmen to sort out the mess. "All this extra work!" he grumbled. "It wears an engine out."

The derailed coach was in the middle of the train, so Skarloey had gone on to the Top Station with the front coaches.

Duncan brought the rear coaches home. He sulked all the way back to the station. "I get no rest! I get no rest!" he muttered.

He arrived back just in time for his own 4 o'clock train. But he was sulky and wouldn't move.

"Come on, we're keeping our passengers waiting," his Driver reminded him.

At last they set off.

Shortly before the next station, they came to a viaduct and Duncan ground to a halt.

"I've had enough. I'm staying here!" he snapped.

And he did, too!

Skarloey had to come down from the Top Station to haul Duncan and his train to the platform.

The passengers were furious. They burst out of the train and told the Drivers, the Firemen and the Guard what a bad Railway it was.

Duncan was still sulky. "Why should I have to work hard, just to pull silly old passengers?" he asked.

But no one was listening to him.

The Thin Controller was waiting for Duncan at the Shed.

"If you won't carry passengers, you won't get polished," he said, sternly.

"I'd rather not be polished if it meant I didn't have to carry passengers," Duncan muttered to himself. But he didn't dare say it loud enough for The Thin Controller to hear!

"I'm ashamed of you, Duncan!" said Skarloey that night. "You should think of your passengers, not yourself."

"Passengers are just nuisances. They're always complaining," replied Duncan.

"That's no way to talk!" said Skarloey. "We need passengers. No passengers means no trains. And no trains means no Railway! I remember when Rheneas saved our Railway because he cared about the passengers."

"Please tell us about it!" said Peter Sam.

Skarloey began: "Rheneas knew we had to keep the trains running or our Railway would have to close. He was often short of steam, but he always struggled on to a station and then rested when he got there.

'I mustn't stop between stations,' he'd say. 'The passengers wouldn't like it.'"

"Pshaw!" huffed Duncan. He had stopped on a viaduct and hadn't cared at all.

"One wet and windy afternoon," Skarloey continued, "when the rails were damp, Rheneas was travelling home with a full train.

'Aaah! I've got cramp!' he groaned, suddenly. And he stopped on the loneliest part of the line.

His Driver examined him. 'Your valve gear has jammed. We need to reach the next station. Do you think you can get us there?' he asked. 'I'll try,' replied Rheneas, bravely."

"So The Thin Controller sanded the rails, some passengers pushed from behind, and Rheneas jerked and began to move forward.

'I'll get there or burst! I'll get there or burst!' Rheneas muttered to himself. And he moved slowly along the track until he finally reached the station.

'Thank you for getting us home,' the passengers said. 'We'll tell all our friends that this is a really fine Railway!'"

"And so you see what a brave engine Rheneas is," said Skarloey to Duncan.

"Thank you for telling us about him," whispered Duncan. "I was wrong. Passengers are important after all!"

The next day, Rheneas came home. The engines greeted him with a chorus of whistles.

But the loudest whistle came from Duncan, who decided he would always put passengers first from then on!

SALTY

Based on *The Railway Series* **by the Rev. W. Awdry**

Illustrations by

Robin Davies and Creative Design

TO THE TRAINS →

This is a story about Salty the Dockyard Diesel. He loved working by the sea, so he didn't think he would like it when I sent him to work at the Quarry. But as it turned out, he was very good with the trucks . . .

Salty was a dockyard diesel who loved telling tales about the sea.

One day, The Fat Controller asked him to come to the Island of Sodor to help finish an important job.

Salty was excited about working there because islands are surrounded by water, so he knew he would never be too far from the sea.

"**A**hoy there, mateys!" said Salty when he arrived at his new job. "I'm here to help you."

"Welcome to Centre Island Quarry," said Mavis.

"A quarry?" said Salty in surprise. "But I'm a dockyard diesel! I'm used to working by the sea."

"You're a quarry diesel now," Mavis said.

Mavis explained that they had three days to complete The Fat Controller's important job. Salty was sad that he wasn't by the sea, but he was a Really Useful Engine, so he got started at once.

"Ah, well," he said. "At least I'll be working with trucks."

"You'd better watch them," said Mavis. "They can be rather tricky."

Bill and Ben, who were also working on the job, didn't think they needed any help – especially from a diesel!

"He won't last five minutes," said Bill.

"Yes, the trucks will trip him up soon enough," replied Ben.

But to their surprise, the trucks gave Salty no trouble at all. "Yo, ho, ho and a bucket of prawns," Salty sang. "The tiller spins . . ."

". . . and the captain yawns," sang the trucks.

Thanks to Salty, by the end of the day the job was almost done. Bill and Ben were very surprised and rather jealous of Salty.

"Here comes Mister Show-off," Ben said when he saw Salty pulling a long line of trucks down the track.

"You have to admit he's got a knack with the trucks," said Mavis.

"Maybe, but Driver says he'll bore the bolts off us with his stories about the sea," huffed Bill.

That night, Salty didn't come into the engine shed. Mavis was worried. She rolled up next to him and asked him what he was doing outside.

"I thought I might catch a little sea breeze," said Salty sadly.

"You really do miss the sea, don't you?" said Mavis.

"Aye," sighed Salty. "I do."

Then Salty told Mavis some of his favourite stories about the sea.

Salty knew the quarry work was important, so the next day he told Bill and Ben his secret for getting the trucks to behave.

"I like working to a musical rhythm," he said. "And so do the trucks. Why don't you give it a try, me hearties?"

Bill and Ben thought singing songs sounded very easy. They decided to try it at once.

But Bill and Ben weren't very good at singing, and they couldn't remember the words of the songs!

Before long, the trucks were causing all sorts of trouble for them. Bill and Ben realised they would never be able to pull as many trucks as Salty. They watched jealously as Salty easily pulled long lines of trucks up and down the tracks.

Later that day, The Fat Controller came to the Quarry. He was surprised to see that his job had been finished.

"Well done!" he said to the engines. "You have worked very hard indeed!"

"We could never have done it without Salty," said Mavis.

Even Bill and Ben had to admit that Salty had helped them finish the job really quickly.

"Now I've got an even bigger job for you, Salty," said The Fat Controller.

"Aye, aye, Sir," said Salty sadly. "What kind of quarry is it this time?"

"Quarry?" said The Fat Controller. "I'm not sending you to a quarry. I want you to work at Brendam Docks!"

"The Docks are right by the sea!" said Salty excitedly.

"Yes, I thought you would like working there," replied The Fat Controller with a smile.

"Oh, thank you, Sir!" said Salty. "Now this reminds me of a time at the Harbour . . ."

And Salty was happily telling sea stories again.

Salty is still working at Brendam Docks.

He is very happy there because he can smell the sea air and watch all the ships sailing past.

The engines on the Sodor Railway love working with Salty and they all admire the fact that he can pull more trucks than any three other engines put together!

STEPNEY

Based on *The Railway Series* by the Rev. W. Awdry

Illustrations by

Robin Davies and Jerry Smith

TO THE TRAINS ⟶

This is a story about Stepney, the Bluebell Engine. One day I sent him to work with Mavis and Toby at the Quarry. I told him to leave there before it got dark, but he didn't listen to me . . .

Stepney usually worked with his friend Rusty. But one day, The Fat Controller said, "I hear you could do with a change of scene, so I want you to help Toby and Mavis at the Quarry."

"Thank you, Sir," Stepney said. "Shall I be away for long?"

"Just today," said The Fat Controller. "And make sure you leave the Quarry before it gets dark. It's very easy to get lost up there."

Stepney soon arrived at the Quarry. Toby and Mavis were waiting for him.

"We're glad you're here to help," said Toby. "We have a lot of work to do."

"Are those my trucks?" asked Stepney.

"Some of them," said Mavis. "There are lots more waiting in the sidings."

"The more the merrier," said Stepney happily.

Stepney really enjoyed working with Mavis and Toby. Later that day, the Quarry Foreman spoke to Stepney's Driver.

"Do you want to take a night special to the building site on the new branch line?" he asked.

"Yes, please," said Stepney's Driver. He had forgotten The Fat Controller's warning about how easy it was to get lost up there in the dark.

Soon night came.

"Be careful, Stepney," said Toby. "It gets very dark on the hillside tracks."

"I will," said Stepney. "Thank you for a lovely day. I do hope I can come back again, soon."

"Watch out," said Mavis. "The line can be rather spooky at night!"

"Thanks for the warning," said Stepney as he puffed away.

Stepney made the delivery. Once everything had been unloaded, he set off for home.

That was when the trouble began. It was very foggy, so Stepney could hardly see where he was going.

"Mavis was right," he said nervously. "Suddenly everything does look rather spooky!"

"There's a signalbox ahead," said his Driver. "The signal is turned to green so someone must be expecting us."

But the points had been accidentally set in the wrong direction. Stepney and his Driver didn't realise that, so they carried on down the wrong track. After a while they realised they didn't know where they were.

"**W**e're lost!" said Stepney's Driver. "I think we should wait here until the fog clears."

Suddenly, they heard a noise.
"What was that?" said Stepney nervously.

As the fog cleared, they realised they were in the scrap yard! Stepney's Driver and Firemen went to find the Foreman.

Two diesels approached Stepney."You'll make good scrap, Stepney," they said.

"Help!" cried Stepney, but no one heard him.

The diesels took Stepney to a smelter's shed. "Goodbye, Stepney," they said.

Stepney looked up nervously. There was a huge grabber moving down towards him. "But I'm not meant to be scrapped!" he cried.

"It's too late now," said the diesels.

But just as the machine was about to grab him, it suddenly stopped. The Fat Controller had turned it off. He had saved Stepney!

"Oh! Thank you, Sir," said Stepney gratefully.

"You are very lucky that I decided to visit this yard tonight," said The Fat Controller sternly. "I can't always be around to save you, Stepney. You have to be more careful!"

Stepney promised to always listen to warnings from then on.

Stepney's Driver was in trouble, too. He had agreed to do the night job without asking The Fat Controller first.

He was very sorry for the trouble he had caused. He promised he would always ask The Fat Controller in future before taking on any jobs.

"I have learnt something useful from this," said Stepney.

"What's that?" asked The Fat Controller.

"I've learnt that there's no place like home!" Stepney said.

"That's very true," said The Fat Controller. "And that's where you are going now."

When Stepney got back to the station, he told Rusty all about his scary time on the foggy hillside and his near-miss at the scrap yard.

Even though it had been exciting to work somewhere different for a while, Stepney realised he was happiest working on The Fat Controller's railway with his good friend, Rusty.

THE END